Carol Stream Public Library
616 Hiawatha Drive
Carol Stream, Illinois   60188

ONE FROG TOO MANY

by Mercer
and Marianna Mayer

DIAL BOOKS FOR YOUNG READERS
New York

Published by Dial Books for Young Readers
A division of NAL Penguin Inc.,
2 Park Avenue, New York, New York 10016
Copyright © 1975 by Mercer and Marianna Mayer. All rights reserved.
Library of Congress Catalog Card Number: 75-6325
Printed in Hong Kong by South China Printing Co.
(b)
8 10 12 14 15 13 11 9 7

For Phyllis Fogelman
who got the ball rolling

. . . Hats off to you

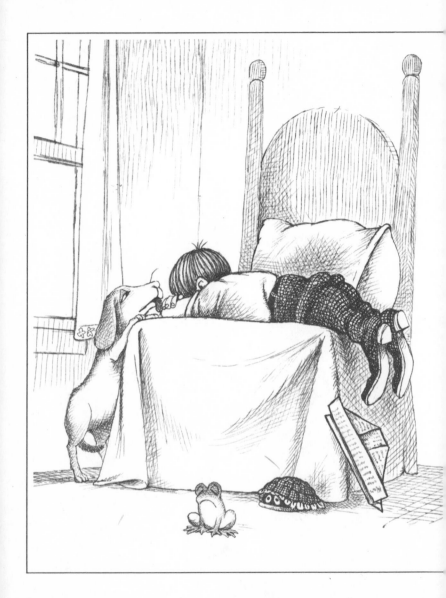